# One of Each

by~ MaryAnn Hoberman

Illustrated by~ Marjorie Priceman

LITTLE, BROWN AND COMPANY

New York   Boston

*For Eric and Andrew Teichman*
*—M.A.H.*

*For Iggy, Miss Tiggy, and Kurt*
*—M.P.*

Text copyright © 1997 by Mary Ann Hoberman
Illustrations copyright © 1997 by Marjorie Priceman

Little, Brown and Company

Hachette Book Group
237 Park Avenue, New York, NY 10017
Visit our website at www.lb-kids.com

Little, Brown and Company is a division of Hachette Book Group, Inc.
The Little, Brown name and logo are trademarks of Hachette Book Group, Inc.

The publisher is not responsible for websites (or their content) that are not owned by the publisher.

First Paperback Edition: September 2000

Library of Congress Cataloging-in-Publication Data
Hoberman, Mary Ann.
    One of each / by Mary Ann Hoberman ; illustrated by Marjorie
Priceman. — 1st ed.
        p.     cm.
    Summary: Oliver Tolliver, who lives alone in his little house with just one of everything, discovers that it is more fun to have two of everything and share with a friend.
    ISBN 978-0-316-36644-1
    [1. Sharing—Fiction.   2. Friendship—Fiction.   3. Stories in rhyme.]   I. Priceman, Marjorie, ill.   II. Title.
PZ8.3.H66On   1997
    [E]—dc20                                                          96-34831
PB: 10  9  8
SC

Manufactured in China

Oliver Tolliver lived all alone
In a little old tumbledown house of his own.
It had one little window and one little door

And one little carpet that covered the floor.
It had one little table and one little chair
And one little closet and one little stair

And one little bedroom and one little bed
With one little pillow for under his head
And one little blanket and one little sheet
And one little bottle to warm up his feet.

In the one little kitchen was one little sink
And one little cupboard all shiny and pink,

And inside the cupboard one pear and one peach,
One plum and one apple, just one, one of each.

*One plum and one apple, one pear and one peach.*
*Just one, only one, simply one, one of each.*

There was one little clock that went *tick-tock, tock-tick*

Over one little fireplace built out of brick.

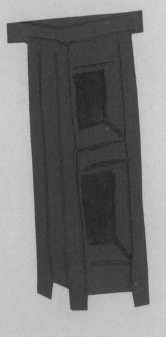

There was one little bookcase with one little book

And one little mirror where someone could look.

And when Oliver Tolliver looked all around,
He smiled with delight, for he liked what he found.
It all seemed so fine, every one-of-each thing,
That he felt just as happy and proud as a king;

And he said to himself, "Why, how nice it would be
If someone could see this, someone besides me.
Why, such a collection would certainly teach
How lovely it is to have one, one of each.

One house with one kitchen, one plum and one peach.
Just one, only one, simply one, one of each."

So Oliver Tolliver carefully dressed
In his one little shirt and his one little vest

And his one little trouser and
one little coat

And his one little tie round his one
little throat,

Put his one little hat on his one little head,

And then Oliver Tolliver cheerfully said,
"I shall walk out my door and go straight down the street
And the very first person I happen to meet
Is the one I will ask to come look and come see.
I wonder which person that person will be."

He started out walking and soon someone came,
A nice-looking person. He asked her her name.
She said it was Peggoty, Peggoty Small,
And said she was pleased to come over to call.

He showed her his stove and his one little sink
And his one little cupboard all shiny and pink,
His chair and his table, his bureau and bed,
And his one little pillow for under his head.
And each time he showed her a one-of-each treasure,
He looked for a sign of enjoyment or pleasure;

But all that she did was repeat the same speech:
"Just one, only one, simply one, one of each?

*Why only one apple? Why only one peach?*
*Why one, simply one, only one, one of each?"*

Oliver Tolliver tried to explain.
He said that the reason was perfectly plain.
If everything fit from the roof to the floor
And each thing was perfect, why bother with more?

But Peggoty answered, "I cannot agree.
It may be for you but it isn't for me.

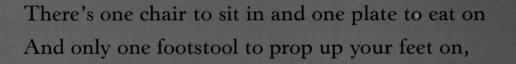

There's one chair to sit in and one plate to eat on
And only one footstool to prop up your feet on,

One cup and one saucer, one pear and one peach,
Oh, dearie, how dreary, with just one of each.

A guest in your one-of-each house does not fit.
It's made for one person and you, sir, are it!
It's perfect for one, sir, if he's on his own,
And so, sir, I'll go, sir, and leave you alone."

Then Oliver Tolliver looked all about.

He looked up and down and he looked in and out.

And he saw that what Peggoty said was quite true:

His one-of-each house was not suited for two.

His one-of-each things never came to an end,

Yet one thing was missing . . . he hadn't one friend.

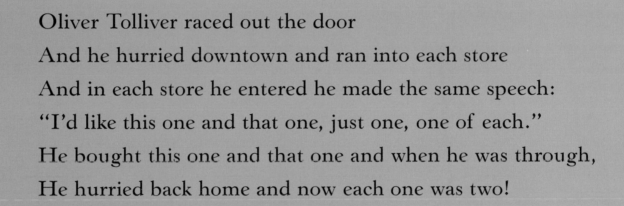

Oliver Tolliver raced out the door
And he hurried downtown and ran into each store
And in each store he entered he made the same speech:
"I'd like this one and that one, just one, one of each."
He bought this one and that one and when he was through,
He hurried back home and now each one was two!

And when he'd arranged all his new things to fit,
He liked what they looked like, he had to admit.
The house was less empty, the kitchen felt new,
The table seemed friendlier set up for two.

Then when he was finished, he called up Miss P.
And invited her over for afternoon tea.
And when she arrived, she cavorted with glee
And she said with delight, "Why, you did this for *me!*

*Why, Oliver dear, you are truly a peach,*
*With two, really two, always two, two of each!"*

They sat at the table in perfect accord,
And they each took a teacup and Peggoty poured,
And they each had a cupcake and when they were done,
Oliver *knew* two was better than one!
Jolly and friendly, more cheerful, more fun!

Then little by little new friends came to call,
And Oliver found he was fond of them all.

What a pity, he thought, there was not any more,
More cupcakes to offer, more tea he could pour.

Then he had an idea as he opened the door,
An idea that he never had thought of before.

He sharpened his knife and he polished his plate,
And he asked his new friends if they kindly would wait.
Then he went to the cupboard and in he did reach
And took out his fruit — there were now two of each…

And he carefully cut them, each plum, peach, and pear,
And he passed round the plate so they all had a share.
And he found as he nibbled the peach, pear, and plum
That they all tasted better when each one had some
And that even though each person's piece might be small,
Eating with friends was the best thing of all.

*And by sharing his pieces of plum, pear, and peach,*
*Each one could have one, still have one, one of each!*